A Dorling Kindersley Book

Project Editor   Caryn Jenner
Art Editor   Jane Thomas
Production   Louise Barratt
Photography   Alex Wilson

First-published in Great Britain in 1996 by
Dorling Kindersley Limited,
9 Henrietta Street, London, WC2E 8PS

Reprinted 1997

Visit us on the World Wide Web at
http://www.dk.com

A CIP catalogue record for this book is available from the British Library.

ISBN 0-7513-5475-9

Colour reproduction by Euroscan, Great Britain
Printed and bound in Italy by L.E.G.O.

Acknowledgements
Dorling Kindersley would like to thank Kier Lusby
and his workshop for making the props.

Dig and Dug with Daisy
TROUBLE with TRUCKS

Caryn Jenner

DORLING KINDERSLEY

LONDON • NEW YORK • STUTTGART • MOSCOW

Dig and Dug had a job to do.

Farmer Stubble had asked them to come to
Merryweather Farm as quickly as they could.

Daisy went, too. "Oh dear," she said.
"Farmer Stubble must be in trouble."

"Whatever the job..." said Dig.
"We'll get it done," said Dug.

 "My tractor has broken down," said Farmer Stubble.
"And I must deliver these crates to Mrs. Green's shop."
"Don't worry," said Dug. "We'll help you."

Dug got the toolbox from the back of his little yellow truck.
Dig tried to fix Farmer Stubble's tractor.
But the tractor wouldn't start.

"Uncle Dug," said Daisy, "let's deliver the fruit in your truck."

"Good idea!" said Dug.

Dig, Dug, and Daisy drove off.
Just when they reached the end of the drive,
GRRRRRRR! roared the engine. But the truck wouldn't go.

"Oh no, we're stuck in a ditch!" said Dug.

"And we've got a flat tyre!" said Dig.
He picked up a spanner. "I'll fix it."
But they didn't have a spare tyre.

"I have an idea," said Dug.

Dug phoned for a tow truck.

"But Uncle Dug, we don't want the fruit towed away," said Daisy.

She opened the gate at the back of the truck. WHOoooMPH! The crates slid out of the truck and into the ditch, followed by the toolbox, a rake, a spade, and a wheelbarrow.

"Oh dear!" said Daisy.

"Come on," said Dig.
He put a crate into
the wheelbarrow and started
off down the road.
"I'm taking these to
Mrs. Green's shop."

"I have a
better idea,"
said
Dug.

Dug arrived with a forklift.
Dig and Dug began stacking the crates.
"Don't stack the crates too high, Dig," warned Daisy.

It was too late. CCRRRAAASH!!!
Down came the crates, scattering fruit everywhere.

"Oh dear," said Dig. He began to rake up the fruit.

"I have a better idea," said Dug.

Dug arrived with a bulldozer.

 SCCCRRRAPE went the bulldozer blade as it pushed the fruit into a big pile.

"We'll need to scoop up all of this fruit now," said Daisy. "I'll do it," said Dig. He picked up some fruit with the spade.

"I have a better idea," said Dug.

Dug arrived with a digger.

BUMPITY-BUMP-BUMP went the fruit as the
metal bucket scooped it up.
"Oh dear," said Dig. "The bucket isn't big enough to
carry all of this fruit to Mrs. Green's shop."

Dug stroked his chin. Dig scratched his head.
What should they do now?

"I have an idea," said Daisy.

When Dig, Dug, and Daisy arrived at the shop, Mrs. Green was surprised to see them delivering her fruit in a GIANT DUMPER TRUCK!

"Whatever the job..." said Dig.
"We'll get it done," said Dug.